alien
encounter

alien
encounter

[BOOK #4 OF THE
alien agent
series]

pamela F. Service

illustrated by mike gorman

darbycreek
Minneapolis

Text copyright © 2010 by Pamela F. Service
Illustrations copyright © 2010 by Lerner Publishing Group, Inc.

Darby Creek
A division of Lerner Publishing Group, Inc.
241 First Avenue North
Minneapolis, MN 55401 U.S.A.

Website address: www.lernerbooks.com

Library of Congress Cataloging-in-Publication Data

Service, Pamela F.
         Alien encounter / by Pamela F. Service ; illustrated by Mike Gorman.
            p.   cm. — (Alien agent)
         Summary: Alien agent Zack travels to Roswell, New Mexico, to search for an alien boy who has
    stolen a spaceship in order to find his missing father who crashed near Roswell in 1947.
         ISBN: 978-0-8225-8873-3 (trade hardcover : alk. paper)
         [1. Extraterrestrial beings—Fiction. 2. Kidnapping—Fiction. 3. Secrets—Fiction. 4. Fathers and
    sons—Fiction. 5. Roswell (N.M.)—Fiction. 6. Science fiction.] I. Gorman, Mike, ill. II. Title.
    PZ7.S4885Al 2010
    [Fic]—dc22   2009020209

Manufactured in the United States of America
3 – SB – 12/15/10

[aLien agent] series

For Mariah Rose
—P. S.

For David, Warren, Steven, and Ms. P.
Thanks for believing in what I did and
never questioning my unique vision.
—M. G.

Prologue

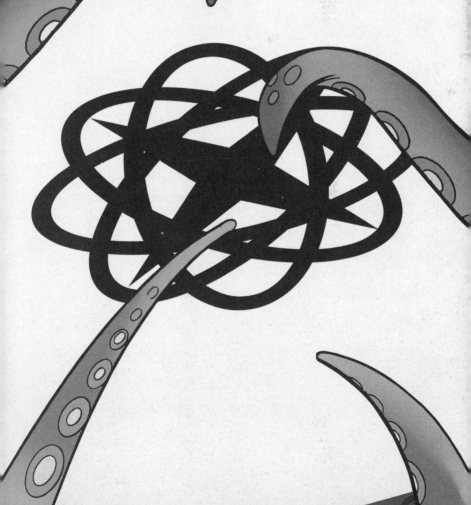

Agent Sorn admired, as always, the sparkling chandelier hanging in the Galactic Union's reception hall. Its many lights reminded her of the stars spangling over her own home planet, near the galactic core. Sighing, Sorn pushed down homesickness. She grabbed a glass of bubbling fuwiji juice from a passing robo-waiter. Turning her attention to the stage, she listened to the Kraktar ambassador talking. He was droning on about the wonders of his watery planet. Sorn giggled. The Kraktarian looked a lot like one of those foods she'd seen on her visits to planet Earth. A pepperoni pizza.

The memory made her hungry. She'd just headed toward the food table when she saw Chief Agent Zythis coming her way. The business-like look in his eyes, all twelve of them, made her want to duck for cover. Too late.

"Agent Sorn," he bubbled. "You look lovely in that shade of orange. It sets off your purple skin and white hair."

"Thanks," she mumbled. "I got this outfit on my last trip to Earth."

"Ah, and Earth is what I want to talk to you about. You know the Galactic Council is considering inviting it to join the Galactic

Union in the near future. If all goes well there, that is."

"Yes," she said cautiously.

"And according to your reports, our planted agent there has been doing surprisingly well. And this is despite his having to be told about his true nature far too early. And he hasn't even completed all his training yet. So I'm sure you'll be as comfortable as I am about giving him one more little assignment."

Sorn groaned silently, but Zythis read her expression. "Now don't worry. It's a simple assignment. No danger involved. In fact, it's so simple and safe you can set it all up remotely. You won't even have to go there."

One of his tentacles handed her a shimmering blue cube. "Here's all the information you need. And don't delay—there is some urgency. Now run along and enjoy this lovely reception."

As her boss swished off, Sorn allowed herself to groan out loud. Enjoy the reception? Now? Sure, she had growing confidence in their young agent. But she had never known anything having to do with Earth that was ever *simple* or *safe*.

I looked through the thick glass of the airplane window at the landscape below. Dry reds and yellows, a desert landscape, like Mars or something. This was Earth, but the sight made me wonder what my own planet was like.

Of course, I still consider Earth my home. I grew up here. Until about a year ago, I thought I was as human as my parents or anyone around. But then I found out I am actually an alien.   Not as in someone from another country but someone from another *planet*.   I'd been planted on Earth as a baby, so I could grow up learning human ways.   The idea was that someday I could act as sort of a representative for the Galactic Union.   It's this big organization of planets.   When they ask Earth to join, I'm supposed to help.

Their plan would have worked smoothly. But some really nasty aliens who didn't want Earth to join the Union tried to kill me.   I had to be told who I really am far earlier than the Galactic Union folks had planned.   After that, they asked me to help with several unexpected problems.   I did.   If I hadn't, Earth people might have become so scared of aliens they wouldn't want to join the Galactic Union when the time came.

Anyway, a few days ago, I had just returned home from one of those secret assignments.   It finally looked like the rest of my summer could be a normal human-kid-type summer.

Wrong.

I was in the kitchen rummaging in the fridge for an afternoon snack. Then my mom came in with the mail. She handed me a fat envelope. I didn't recognize the return address. But when I opened it, I discovered that I had won an essay contest I had entered. My essay, "What I'd Do If I Met a Real Alien," had won an all-expenses-paid trip. One parent and I would travel to Roswell, New Mexico, for their annual UFO festival.

The problem was that I had never entered any contest.

But I knew enough to recognize this was the Galactic Union messing with my life again. So I acted happy in front of my mom. Then I escaped upstairs to my room. I dropped into the swivel desk chair. Trying to calm myself for a moment, I looked at my movie and music posters on the wall. But the familiar pieces of my life were falling away so fast lately that this didn't work anymore. Taking a deep breath, I switched on my computer.

Sure enough, there was an incoming message from my boss, Agent Sorn. Locking my bedroom door, I made the coded entry. Sorn's smiling purple face popped up on my screen. It was still a shock to see her not wearing her human-skin-color disguise. Her hair was its usual startling white. Her smile looked kind of apologetic.

"Zack, you should have your packet now. I'm sure you'd like a little explanation."

I only grunted.

"Zack, I'm really sorry to do this to you again. You shouldn't have to deal with these things until you are older and better trained. But the Galactic Union is stretched awfully thin in your sector of the galaxy. You are our only agent on the ground there. And if you don't solve this crisis, the whole thing could fall apart."

I tried not to look as annoyed as I felt. So much for my hopes of a normal human summer. Still, my curiosity stirred a little. "So, okay, what's this big crisis?"

Sorn raked long fingers through her hair. It stood up like a polar porcupine's. "Have you ever heard of the so-called flying saucer crash in Roswell, New Mexico, back in 1947?"

I thought a moment. "Yeah, I think I saw a TV program about it once." I didn't remember much. That was before I had any personal interest in aliens, after all. "But didn't it turn out to be a hoax or something?"

"Your government would like you to believe that. They put out several cover-up stories. Said it was really a weather balloon and such. But, no, it was real. A real alien ship did crash."

"Whose?" I knew enough by then to realize there were nearly as many types of aliens as stars in the sky.

"Nythians. The Galactic Union had placed Earth off limits. They warned interstellar travelers to stay away. No one was to interfere before Earth's civilization had reached a higher level of technology and stability. But we didn't have enough personnel to really enforce it. The Nythians are kind and peaceful but very private. They're not known for joining groups or obeying rules. They're a very curious people too. They'd become interested in Earth and concerned about it getting nuclear weapons. A number of Nythian ships visited Earth in the 1940s and 1950s. Some were seen, but most humans didn't take the sightings seriously."

Sorn glanced aside at what might be another screen. Then she looked back at me. "I'll send you more background information. But the big problem came in July of 1947. One Nythian ship was damaged in an electrical storm. It crashed near Roswell. Several civilians found the crash site first, and word leaked out. But soon the American military whisked away the wreckage and the bodies of the crew. Then they tried to hush things up."

I was stunned. "So the government *does* know about the existence of aliens!"

"Actually, only a small group knew the truth. Other people in the government believed the denials. Evidence would have been slim because Nythian bodies turn to dust shortly after death. A crashed ship is programmed to automatically self-destruct. Crew members have only a short time to cancel that."

This was interesting, but I didn't see how I fit in. "So what's the problem? That was long ago. What does it matter now?"

Sorn gave a tired little laugh. "We didn't think there *was* a problem until recently. Oh, some humans latched onto the story of a UFO crash and short, bug-eyed aliens. For some reason, they called them little green men. Of course, Nythians aren't green. Books and magazines about UFOs popped up. Roswell became the center for UFO believers and hokey alien souvenirs. They now even hold an annual UFO festival there. Quite harmless, really."

Sorn was becoming annoyingly dramatic, stretching the story out like this. "So what changed?"

She sighed. "Recently we learned about a Nythian child named Tu, the son of one of that ship's crew. He has—what's the Earth phrase? Yes, developed 'a bee in his bonnet.' He believes his father somehow survived the crash and is still on Earth. Now it seems this kid has stolen a ship. He's headed toward

Earth. According to his worried mother, his idea is to go to Roswell while they are having their festival. He hopes to learn if there were any survivors and find out if his father might be one."

Something wasn't making sense to me. "Sorn, that was more than sixty years ago. He wouldn't be a kid anymore. And even if his dad survived the crash, he probably wouldn't be alive now."

Sorn shook her head. "We're not talking about humans here, Zack. Nythians mature very slowly. They have very long lives. But whatever the son may want to believe, it is very unlikely that anyone survived that crash. Nor could they have stayed alive and undetected since then. The real danger is that the young Nythian will get himself caught. Nythians tend to be rather naive and trusting. If the government or UFO enthusiasts get their hands on a real space alien, who knows what would happen? It could certainly destroy the Galactic Union's plans. We hope for a gradual introduction to the idea that other planets are inhabited."

I was beginning to get the drift of this. "So my job is . . . what? Find this kid and tell him to go home?"

She smiled. Her amethyst-colored eyes actually twinkled. Her species can do that. "That's right. You've become quite a capable agent, Zack, even though your training isn't complete. You're clever and resourceful. I'm sure you'll be able to carry this out. And whichever parent you choose to go with you won't even catch on."

I just grunted.

Sorn looked concerned. "I do hate dumping all these tasks on you. But this is very important, Zack. So much depends on you. You don't mind *too* much, do you?"

I managed to smile and shake my head.

"Good." She sounded relieved. "And anyway, this is really a simple assignment. And it also gives you a fun little vacation."

Sorn is a nice person. The Galactic Union seems to be a fine outfit with a mission I'm proud to be part of. But I have *got* to learn not to buy statements like that.

Simple and fun? Yeah, right.

CHAPTER TWO

So here I was, a few days later, flying over New Mexico. The bleak desert and dramatic mesas were slowly giving way to scrubby grassland. Less dramatic, but I didn't want drama. I wanted an assignment that could be done quickly and easily. Then maybe my dad and I could take advantage of this free trip. Maybe we could actually do some fun vacation stuff.

Crammed into those cramped airline seats, my dad was sitting beside me reading a travel magazine. Because he's a teacher, it's easier for him to get away in the summer than for my mom. And he'd seemed really happy to be coming along. He was proud of me for supposedly writing that winning essay. Plus he was looking forward to having some father-and-son time. The idea was that I'd spend a few days at the festival, while he did other tourist stuff. Then maybe we'd rent some camping gear and go off roughing it for a while.

I glanced at him sideways and fought down a wave of guilt. He's a great dad even if he's not my real father. I'd never known my real parents. I didn't even know if my species had children the same way. No, these were my parents as far as I was concerned. They'd never even told me I was adopted. And they had no clue about what I really was. Once I'd learned the truth about myself, I had wished that I could tell them. All of it. But I was supposed to keep my real identity a secret from everyone on Earth as long as possible.

Despite that, I still half wanted to tell them. I was also half afraid to. Learning what I was hadn't changed my feelings toward them. But would it change their feelings toward me? They thought they'd adopted a human baby, after all. Frankly, I was afraid to know that answer.

Better to just focus on my mission here. That should be challenging enough.

As we flew in over Roswell, the town looked a lot bigger than I'd imagined. Finding one person who didn't want to be found in a town that size would not be easy. According to the Roswell website, 50,000 people were expected to attend the UFO festival. I had to find visitor number 50,001.

After we landed, we picked up our luggage and took a taxi to our hotel. I unpacked my secret equipment, which looked pretty pathetic. One was a baseball-type hat. It had a black diamond in a blue circle. The Nythian coat of arms. Then came a T-shirt printed front and back with a bright green message in Nythian. Basically it said, "Hi Tu, I'm Zack, a friend sent here to help you. Please introduce yourself." That was it. I was supposed to wear those things everywhere during the festival. The idea was that Tu would see the message and say hello. Kind of a long shot, if you ask me. But nobody had.

My dad and I were both tired after a day of airports and airplanes. We ate dinner at a Mexican restaurant and turned in early. The next day, Dad decided to enjoy his love for bird-watching. He rented a car to drive to a nearby bird sanctuary. I was glad I didn't have to go along. It seems a little rude (to say nothing of boring) to spend hours sitting still, staring at birds. The poor things are just trying to live their lives.

After Dad left on his outing, I put on my Nythian gear. Leaving the air-conditioned hotel, I stepped into the furnace heat of a New Mexico July. As I walked down Main Street, I showed off hat and shirt to all the locals, tourists, and festivalgoers. No one gave me a second glance. But I had plenty to look at.

Shops, restaurants, and offices all had green, inflatable aliens in their windows. Every other shop was pushing UFO and alien souvenirs. T-shirts, mugs, refrigerator magnets, and boxes of fudge all sported green, pointy alien faces with big slanted eyes. Even the globes on the street lamps were pale green glass with dark, slanted eyes painted on them. Theme songs from various space movies blasted from every door.

The whole thing made me feel weird. People were having fun, and the whole town was making money off a crash that had killed several people. Alien people, sure, but people. Like me.

I had never felt so alien before. I was hit with the crazy feeling that everybody would see what I really was. Then they'd start panicking. But nobody did. The weird feeling faded, and I tried to concentrate on my job.

The UFO museum was in an old movie theater. I picked up a program of festival events. Where would a young Nythian go to learn more about the UFO crash and what might have happened to the crew?

Events like glow-in-the-dark disc golf, balloon rides, and a corn maze might be fun.

But they probably wouldn't be very helpful. There were lots of talks by various noted "UFO-ologists." They covered things like crop circles in England, aliens shown in ancient art, and UFO studies in China. I crossed them off, since they didn't deal with the Roswell crash.

There were also talks on Roswell topics. I spent much of the long, very hot day trudging up and down Main Street to three buildings. In them, talks were being held in overcrowded, under-air-conditioned rooms. The talks were interesting enough, but mostly I just wanted to be seen. I tried to stand near the front of the meeting rooms. As I looked over the crowds, I hoped someone would be looking at me. No luck.

I was beginning to think my shirt might as well say, "Eat at Joe's" for all the effect it was having. Discouraged, I left after a mid-afternoon talk on government cover-ups. I scanned the schedule for another likely topic. A voice behind me suddenly grabbed my attention.

"Nice shirt."

I spun around. The speaker didn't look like a young Nythian. He was tall. Nythians are short. His skin was a sunburned pink. Nythians are a pale bluish gray. And while Nythians are hairless, this guy had a bristly red mustache. Beneath the mustache, his smile looked forced and hungry.

"Eh, yeah. Thanks," I muttered.

"All that writing, kid, it's pretty fancy stuff. What is it?"

I looked down at the curves, squiggles, and angular lines marching across my chest. "Oh, nothing. It's just some made-up stuff. It's supposed to be an alien language."

"But what is it supposed to say?"

"Nothing. It's just gibberish. Something that's supposed to look cool. Sorry, I've got to go. Promised to meet my dad." I hadn't, of course. But this guy was beginning to bug me.

I slipped into a hall crowded with vendors and shoppers. Little kids were everywhere. Some were getting their faces painted. Others were buying balloons that looked like green alien faces. Another group was having long balloons twisted into alien shapes. Serious-looking people were pouring over books on UFOs, the occult, and other out-there topics. One author had a line eagerly waiting for his autograph. His book was *Did Aliens Build the Pyramids?*

I don't think so! Give humans some credit.

A couple of times I glimpsed Mustache Man in the crowd. Was he following me? No, I'd just been hearing too much about conspiracies and cover-ups. Most of the speakers and books were into conspiracies. Still, one time when I knew he could see me, I bought a T-shirt. I wanted to let Mustache Man know I just like weird T-shirts. This one said, "Welcome to Roswell" with a little, waving green alien.

I also got a really cool pair of sunglasses. They had big, slanted lenses like alien eyes. And I bought a green, smiling alien thimble for my mom. She collects them. Thimbles, that is.

After stuffing these into my backpack, I looked around. No Mustache Man. I was just slipping out a side door when a chilling thought struck me. This was the only person who had even blinked at my T-shirt. He couldn't be a Nythian, even a heavily disguised one. He couldn't read their writing. But could he be some other type of alien? I knew all too well that not all aliens are friendly.

Get real, I told myself. Agent Sorn hadn't said anything about other aliens being involved in this. And why would they be? No, I was getting as paranoid as some of these people giving the lectures.

Once outside, I bought a cardboard tray of nachos from a sidewalk vendor. I messily ate them on a park bench. But I still kept an eye out for Mustache Man just in case. Then, boldly flashing my T-shirt, I headed off to the next event that sounded promising.

Throughout that day, I mingled with thousands of people. Some were serious UFO fanatics. Some were just having fun. But as far as I could tell, there was no scared alien kid on a wild goose chase. No one looking for a father who'd probably died in the New Mexico desert more than sixty years ago.

Back at the hotel, my dad had just returned from a day of bird-watching. We went to dinner at one of those all-you-can-eat Chinese buffets. (I can eat a lot.) He told me about all the exciting bird species he'd seen. Exciting to some, maybe. I tried to pretend equal excitement over what I'd done that day. But I was feeling more and more annoyed that I couldn't tell him what I was really doing. Still, I cringed when I imagined how that conversation would go.

Returning to our hotel room, I flopped down on my bed and soaked up the air conditioning. A sharp knock on the door interrupted my dad enthusiastically outlining his plans for visiting museums and such. Since my bed was closest to the door, I got up and went to open it. I wish I hadn't.

Mustache Man stood there smiling his hungry animal smile. He pushed his way in before I could even think of slamming the door. Whipping out a leather billfold, he flipped it open to a very official-looking badge.

"Sorry to bother you two." He didn't sound the least bit sorry. "I'm Major Garrett, Army Intelligence. I just have a few questions to ask you."

My dad stood up looking confused. "What could you possibly have to ask us?"

"It's about your son's T-shirt. Where'd he get it?"

"The contest people sent it to him."

"What contest people?"

I stepped in. "Look, I won an essay contest. The festival organizers sent me the shirt as a prize."

"Is this true, mister?" Major Garrett asked my dad.

"Of course it is! Now I have a question for you. Why are you harassing us about my son's chosen attire?"

"Sorry, sir, that's classified."

Suddenly something came back to me from one of the lectures I'd sat through. "I bet I know what your problem is. It's the writing, isn't it? The books on the Roswell crash all say there was writing on the wreck. One of the witnesses copied some. But it's published in the books, so it can't be classified. The people who printed the T-shirt must have used those symbols. Then they made up others to go with them."

"No, there's more . . . ," the major began. Then he stopped. I had a cold feeling I knew what he'd started to say. There must have been more writing on the wrecked spaceship. Writing that the witness hadn't remembered or published. But Garrett couldn't say that without admitting that there really had been a crashed UFO. And I couldn't call him on it without admitting that I knew this was real alien writing.

So I just smiled innocently. Garrett smiled knowingly. And my dad, who wasn't smiling at all, stepped in.

"So your questions are answered. I don't know what you're suspicious about, but my son is *not* your suspect. Now you can just go harass someone else."

Major Garrett scowled again at my shirt. Then forcing a smile, he handed me his card "in case I had any reason to talk to him." With a fake-sounding apology, he left.

At that moment, I felt so proud of my dad I could burst.

"Well done, Dad!" I said once the door closed.

"You'd think the military had more pressing security issues to worry about. Still, maybe it would be smart if you didn't wear that shirt tomorrow."

A flash of panic. "No! I mean, I think I have to. It's a freedom-of-speech thing now. Besides, the festival people were really happy to see me wearing it."

That last part wasn't true, of course. The festival people had nothing to do with this shirt. I really hated always lying to my dad. I hurried on.

"You know, some people take this UFO thing really seriously. It's like a religion or something. But most are just having fun with it."

"And how about you? Are you having fun here, Zack?"

"Oh, yeah." Another lie—well, partially. "And are you having fun with your birdwatching and going to museums?"

"Absolutely. It's an ideal vacation for me. But if the festival is going to do something to honor your winning essay, I'd love to be there."

My mind skipped wildly over a new set of lies. "Well, yeah . . . that'd be great. But the festival organizers are really busy . . . eh, organizing the festival. I met some at the sign-in table. They were happy to see me and all. But they haven't planned anything formal. They just said to enjoy my visit."

Dad chuckled. "Well, I certainly wouldn't want to be in charge of organizing this craziness. There's a festival schedule posted in the hotel lobby. It says there's a nighttime parade tomorrow night.   I'd rather enjoy seeing that."

"Sure, I'd like to see that too."   It didn't sound very helpful, but it did sound fun.

"Splendid!   Let's both meet back here in plenty of time tomorrow to see it together. And call me on your cell phone if there's any other festival events you think I ought to take in.   I was considering visits to the local history museum and a couple of historic houses tomorrow, but I can do those another time."

"Nah.   You do the historic stuff.   I'll do the weird stuff.   We'll compare notes when we get together for the parade."

I kept trying to sound all upbeat. Later, when I slid into my hotel bed, I was strung tight with worry.   The festival would only last two more days.   What if I never found the Nythian kid?   I suppose it was better that Mustache Man had turned out to be a human and not some mysterious bad alien.   But what if some government guy like Major Garrett found the kid?   And what if that guy took Tu to some secret military base to question him? Or what if some semi-crazy UFO fanatic found Tu and splashed it all over the grocery store tabloids? Either way, it could destroy the Galactic Union's whole plan.

And it would be my fault.

CHAPTER THREE

Next morning with my dad safely off seeing sights, I sat on the end of my bed. I studied the schedule of events in the brochure. Hot air balloon rides. A skateboard contest. A play at the community theater. Hardly. A lecture on UFOs in Hollywood movies didn't sound promising either. Neither did the one about UFO sightings in Turkey.

Frustrated, I finally decided to walk back to the UFO museum. It was already hot. My special T-shirt was sticking to me before I'd gone half a block. That got me wondering what the Nythians' home planet was like. Would this kid be hot and miserable? Or would he find it chilly? And what about *my* home planet? I'd noticed that my dad had picked up a little sunburn yesterday. I never sunburned. Mosquitoes don't like me either. You'd think that I—or someone—would have noticed things like this before. But I guess you believe what you expect to believe. Everyone believed I was human. So had I—once.

Again, my shirt didn't cause any reactions on Roswell's crowded sidewalks. Now I kept an anxious eye open not only for possible Nythians but also for government agents. Nothing on any score. At the UFO museum, I wandered again through an exhibit of enlarged newspaper articles. Some were about the Roswell incident. Others included accounts by various witnesses. A slide show of UFO photos by amateur photographers wasn't very convincing. The photos could be easily faked.

Again I checked out the book stalls. I picked up a book on developing your psychic power. The Galactic Union training through my doctored computer had included that. The results were mixed and rather unnerving. It's one thing as a kid to dream about having superpowers. It's another to discover you actually have some. Even worse is the fact that the powers are hard to understand *and* to control. Most of the time, I was happiest when I didn't think about the odd things, physical and mental, that I could do.

Trudging back up Main Street, I stopped at a burger place built like a flying saucer. I had a Space Burger and an ET Shake. They tasted like every other hamburger and milkshake. As I was leaving, I saw Major Garrett crossing the street and heading my way. I spun around. No other nearby exit. Not for customers anyway. Ducking around the counter, I dodged the waitresses' protests and the cooks' flailing spatulas. Finally I burst out the back kitchen door into an alley.

That James Bond–type move might have been stupid, I told myself. Probably Garrett had just wanted lunch. Still, he clearly knew something more than he should. And he suspected that I did as well. I kept to the side streets and alleys

Thoroughly hot and sticky, I finally reached the convention center. I was pleased to see two things. First, I didn't seem to have been followed. Second, the next talk I wanted to attend was in the art museum across the plaza. I'd gone to a talk there yesterday. That room definitely had the best air conditioning. No, my native planet was probably not a hot desert one.

The lecture hall was already crowded. I had to sit in the back. From there, I couldn't see the speakers or the slides very well. Still, the talk grabbed my attention. It was about the rumors, accounts, and arguments about the UFO crash. The speaker discussed what happened to the supposed wreck of the spaceship and the bodies of the crew. Witnesses said they'd seen weird bodies and wreckage. They saw some at the crash site and others at the Roswell Air Force Base where everything had supposedly been taken. These were responsible-sounding witnesses. There were soldiers, a nurse, the local funeral director. Some of those people later disappeared or took back their statements, maybe under government pressure. Then the government changed its story several times about what had happened.

This was all pretty interesting. But one thing really caught me. Some witnesses had said that one of the aliens was still alive when they found the crash. Some said it was also alive at the Air Force base hospital. What happened after that was lost in military secrecy.

That got me to thinking. Was it possible that this Nythian kid's dad really had survived, for a while anyway? Of course, he probably couldn't still be alive after all this time. But still, that put a little different spin on my mission. Maybe this wasn't just an alien kid with a wild imagination. If I found him, should I just send him home?

I was lost in these thoughts, when the talk ended. The crowd began filing out of the lecture hall. Suddenly something caught my attention. A voice.

"Nice shirt."

I spun around. It wasn't Major Garrett. It was a short kid with a floppy hat, dark glasses, gloves, and baggy shirt and pants. The voice continued in English with an odd accent. "If you can help me, I really do need help."

"Tu?" I asked, hardly believing this was working.

"Yes. My dad is alive, I know that. But it is harder to locate him than I thought it would be. Can you truly help?"

I just stared down at him a moment. Then grabbing him by a skinny shoulder, I pulled him out of the stream of people. Sorn had been right about Nythians. Too naive and trusting. "Let's talk somewhere more private."

Steering him through several galleries in the museum, we stopped in a small room. The art in there was too ugly for many people to want to see. We were the only people there. I knelt down, so we could be eye to eye. Not that I could see his eyes. His outfit pretty well covered him up. But the patches of skin I glimpsed did look distinctly gray.

"Tu," I said slowly, "I was sent here by the Galactic Union. They are afraid that the natives might find out you're here. That could cause lots of trouble."

"But my father is here. I have got to help him get home."

"The Galactic Union people believe the entire crew was killed in that crash," I said gently.

"You just heard the lecture person say that one crew member survived. That was my dad."

Maybe, but not likely. I didn't want him to get his hopes up. "Tu, there are a lot of things said at this festival that aren't necessarily true. Even if someone did survive for a while, it might not be your dad. And the government was being so secret about everything. Who knows where they may have taken the guy.

Besides that was years and years ago. It's not likely he would still be alive."

Tu crossed his arms, looking like a stubborn human kid. "My dad is. I can feel it. And he is not very far away. But there are so many people here. The place is so confusing. I can not find him."

His voice trembled a little. Taking off his dark glasses, he looked into my eyes. His own eyes were large, dark, and slanting. They were very like the alien eyes that decorated half the things in this town. "Will you help me? I miss my dad so much."

That plea jabbed into me. Imagine not seeing your father for more than sixty years. Knowing he was alive somewhere. Probably in danger. Maybe hurt. Of course, it was probably just wishful thinking on this kid's part. But I couldn't turn him down flat.

"Okay. We'll talk about it. There are a lot of different possibilities here. But we'd better go somewhere more private than this. We can't risk anyone finding out about you."

I stood up and turned toward the gallery entrance. Someone was walking toward us. Someone who wasn't looking at the paintings. Major Garrett. His toothy smile bristled up the ends of his mustache. "I knew it! That shirt's not gibberish. You were communicating with the lost alien. And here, at last, I have him!"

Tu tried to jam his dark glasses back on. Garrett lunged. He ripped off glasses, hat, and baggy shirt. Grabbing the kid's hand, he managed only to pull off a glove. There before us stood a little alien. Bluish gray skin. Skinny body. Long arms. Four-fingered hands. He was everything the reports talk about. Except that his expression was that of a really scared kid.

Without thinking, I thumped Garrett with a special blow. The Galactic Union had been trying to teach me self-defense moves through the computer. I don't think I did it quite right, but Garrett did grunt and sprawl to the floor. Grabbing Tu's hand, I sprinted for the room's exit.

There weren't many other people in the museum now. We ran through a lot of rooms before we found the main doors. All the while, I was trying to cover up my obviously alien companion. I flopped my own hat on his head. Then I yanked the T-shirt I'd bought out of my backpack. People were staring, so I didn't take the time to pull it on him. As we ran, I wrapped the shirt around his shoulders.

At last, we burst into the sunshine. There were people everywhere. The crowd was thick toward the center of the plaza. Maybe we could get lost there. My backpack was now hanging from one arm. Fumbling in it, I pulled out the alien-eyes dark glasses. I stuck them on Tu. Charging into the crowd, we wormed our way between people. Maybe we'd disappear before Garrett could get on our trail.

Suddenly, we stumbled into a clearing in the crowd. We smacked against the edge of a low wooden platform. Tu's hat, glasses, and T-shirt wrap went flying. I scrambled onto the platform. It looked like it had just been set up for some event. Grabbing up the bits of Tu's disguise, I finally straightened up and looked around. The platform—no—the stage was surrounded with people. They were all looking at us.

A man in a flashy purple suit frowned at us. "Sorry, the costume contest is almost over. No late entrants."

"Eh . . . yeah, sorry," I spluttered, trying to cover up Tu again.

Just then a tubby woman scurried up. She wore a bright orange dress, wiggly antennas, and a badge saying Judge. Clucking like a hen, she clapped a hand sparkling with rings on Tu's shoulder. She pulled him up onto the stage.

"No, we can't disqualify this kid. Look at the great costume! Have you ever seen a better Roswell alien costume?"

CHAPTER FOUR

The crowd at the costume contest cheered. Even the other contestants standing on the stage applauded. One guy dressed like a *Star Trek* Klingon bowed grandly to Tu. A girl wearing a spangly bikini and two extra arms used one of her real hands to shake Tu's.

"I agree," she cried. "He's the winner!"

Great disguise, I thought. But not a great situation.

"Thanks," I said loudly. "My kid brother has been working really hard on his costume. But he can't really win. Our parents didn't say we could do this. We'll get in big trouble. Thanks, but we've got to go! Keep on with your contest."

Clutching the discarded clothes, I grabbed Tu's hand. We charged for the down ramp at the other end of the stage. Pushing our way through the surprised crowd, we ducked through the first door we saw. There weren't many people inside the convention center because of the costume contest outside. Quickly I led us to the men's room. I headed for the roomy stall at the end meant for guys in wheelchairs.

Locking the door, I leaned against it and sighed.

Tu looked up at me. "You said there would be dangers if people saw me. But they *liked* me. That was fun!"

I shook my head. "They liked you because they thought you were a kid in a cool costume. If they knew you were for real, they'd freak."

"I do not understand."

"That's for sure. Come on. Cover up again. We'll find someplace more private to talk."

Soon Tu was disguised in my hat, new T-shirt, and alien-eyes glasses. I turned my own T-shirt inside out. I told him to keep his gray four-fingered hands tucked in his pockets. Then we walked out of the bathroom and into the exhibit hall. Tu wanted to look at everything. But finally I managed to steer him into a small empty meeting room that had nothing interesting to look at. We plunked ourselves into a couple of folding chairs at a long conference table. Tu looked up at me expectantly.

"Okay, one of the reasons we need to keep you secret is so we don't freak out people. But another one is that guys like Major Garrett back there would just love to catch you."

"But they did not catch my dad," Tu said confidently. "Or if they did, he got away."

"How can you be so sure?"

"I just know. Do you not know where your family is?"

"Well, I know where they probably are. My dad's probably still at some historic site around here. My mom's back home somewhere. In her office maybe."

"But you can not *feel* them?"

"Well, no. Can you?"

Tu nodded his big head on his very skinny neck. "It is kind of vague, though. I have always known he was alive somewhere on Earth. I have been planning to sneak here for years. That is why I learned your language. I watched a great many of your satellite video broadcasts. But now that I am here, all I can sense is that he is too. He is somewhere fairly close. Everything is so strange and muddled, though. I can not locate him exactly."

Tu didn't have much in the way of lips. But what he had were quivering.

"Okay," I said quickly, patting his arm. "You may be right. From what Major Garrett said when he grabbed you, he seemed to think you are the lost alien. That might mean that one of the crash victims *did* get away. Maybe Garrett was looking for him."

Tu sat up straighter. "Ah. That nasty man thinks that I am my father. So that proves my father is alive!"

"Well, maybe." I thought a moment. My job had just gotten twice as complicated. Instead of one out-of-place alien to get off this planet, there might be two. "Is there some sort of place around here where your father might be hiding?"

Tu hung his head. "I have tried to learn that by going to all those exhibits and talks. But it has not helped much. I can not even pick up a clear sense of where he is. There are so many minds around here. The air is so full of thoughts and feelings. It is a confused jumble."

Yes, I thought. Fifty thousand festival visitors and many locals. That could kind of clog the psychic airwaves. "So maybe we should go somewhere quiet. A place where there aren't so many minds working. Maybe my dad could drive us out to that bird sanctuary he went to. I'm supposed to meet him soon at the hotel to see tonight's parade. I could say you're a friend I met here who..."

Just then the door opened. A chubby woman in lots of floaty shawls swept in. "Oh, you two are early for my talk. But you'll love it! All about communicating with aliens through astrology. What are your star signs, by the way?"

We both stood up. I sputtered, "St . . . star signs? Oh, like in horoscopes. Yeah, your talk really sounds great. But we were just resting here till it's time to meet my dad. That's now."

Taking Tu's long cool hand, I hurried out a door on the other side of the meeting room. It led to a service corridor. That led to an unused kitchen. That led to another corridor and finally to a door to the outside.

Keeping a wary eye out for Major Garrett, we threaded our way through parking lots, side streets, and alleys. Finally we weren't near people. I asked Tu some questions.

"So you stole . . . borrowed a spaceship and flew here. Where did you park it?"

He smiled. "I flew around for a while trying to find a hidden landing spot. There is a river east of town. And past that are some cliffs and lakes but no people. I hid the ship there. I will be relieved, though, when we find my father. He can fly the ship back. I am not a very good pilot yet."

"So how did you get from the hiding place to town? It sounds like a long way."

He patted a bulge on the utility belt he was wearing. "I brought an antigravity pack. I waited until night then just skimmed along over the ground until I got to town. I had my Earth disguise ready. It was working good until that nasty man tore it off."

"Yes, it was." I was impressed. The kid must have been planning this for years. The least I could do was go along with him for now. And maybe his dad really was out there somewhere.

On our way, we made one stop at a café. We bought a couple of root beer floats. I chose an isolated table. Quietly I told him a little about myself, my alien-agent job and all. Tu told me something about his home planet.

It wasn't nearly as hot as New Mexico in July. I was a little worried about whether or not Nythians could eat our food. But Tu took a tiny device from his belt and pointed it at the frosty glass. When it beeped, he happily took a big sip through the straw. A handy poison detector, I guess.

When we reached the hotel, it was nearly the time I'd agreed to meet Dad. On the way up to our room in the elevator, I practiced the story I'd tell him about Tu. How we'd made friends. How his mom was busy as one of the festival organizers. She'd asked if he could watch the parade with us. But I didn't know how to arrange getting us out to the bird sanctuary. Maybe we didn't have to go that far out of town to get away from so much psychic noise. Once my dad was asleep, maybe I could meet Tu in the hotel lobby. Maybe we could just walk out of town a ways. This was cattle ranching country, plenty of open land. Then I wondered if cow thoughts would confuse the psychic scene.

Leaving the elevator, we walked down the carpeted hallway to our room. I was just pulling out the key card, when a feeling of dread slammed into me. I did not want to open that door. Confused, I shook my head. Could I be that worried about what to tell my dad?

No, it was something else. Something worse. It involved my dad, but it had nothing to do with what lies I'd have to tell him.

Slipping the key card into the slot, I jerked the door open. "Dad," I called. "I'm back." But I knew he wasn't there. Something else was, though. A mess.

The chair by the table was tipped over. The contents of both our suitcases were strewn around the room. My dad's cell phone lay smashed at the base of the wall. It looked like it had been thrown there.

The map and guidebooks had been swept off the table. But there was no note. Nothing reassuring like, "Went to the lobby to get some gum. Back soon. Dad." No message at all. But the room gave its own message.

I sank weakly down on one of the beds. Tu stood beside me with a questioning look. I cleared my throat. "My dad's gone. I think he's been kidnapped."

CHAPTER FIVE

Tu's big dark eyes blinked. "Kidnapped? By whom? Why?"

I knew the answer but wished I didn't. "It's got to be that Major Garrett. He thinks my dad knows something about the Roswell wreck. It's because of my shirt with the Nythian writing. But Dad doesn't know a thing. He doesn't know about the crash, not even about me being an alien. An innocent man, my own father, has been kidnapped by bad guys. And it's my fault!"

Tu sat down beside me. He was so light he hardly made a dent in the flowery bedspread.

"It is not a matter of fault. It is a matter of what to do now."

I looked at the kid, wondering if Nythians were as logical as the *Star Trek* Vulcans. But he was right. This was no time for me to freak. "Right. What do we do?"

"We have two missing fathers now," he said after a moment. "But most probably yours is in greater danger. We go after him first."

"Okay, but I have no idea where he is."

"You must. He is your father. In what direction do you feel he has been taken?"

I shook my head. "But he's not my real father."

"That does not matter. He raised you, did he not?"

"Sure, but I can't sense people the way you do. Humans don't do that."

"You are not human."

He was right. I was an alien with alien powers that I was just beginning to explore. But sensing people's psychic aura or whatever? Hardly.

I stared blankly at the mess on the floor. But wait. How had I known there was something wrong even before I opened the hotel room door? My computer lessons from Agent Sorn had been trying to develop my mental powers. I'd sort of blown the whole thing off as being just too weird. Too weird and scary. But more things like that had been working than I'd wanted to admit.

Standing up, I paced around the room. I randomly picked up bits of my dad's clothes. Then I righted the chair and sat in it. "Okay, so if I want to start sensing my dad's whereabouts, what do I do?"

Tu got up and walked over to me. He put his long cool fingers on my shoulder. "Make yourself calm. Close your eyes. Do not think about anything except your father. Cool, deep thoughts. Empty out everything else."

My agent training instructions were always saying things like that. Empty your mind. Do you have any idea how hard it is to do that?

My mind's always buzzing with stuff. Pictures of things I'd done that day. Plans for what I'd do next. Snatches of conversations I'd had or wished I'd had. Pieces of annoying music. My mind was like a garbage pail.

But, okay, empty it. I pictured taking out my mind like I took out the weekly kitchen scraps. I emptied it into the compost bin. Then I washed out the pail with a hose. A jet of cool, cleansing water. Cool and deep. Breathing deeply, I let thoughts of my dad float on the top. Slowly they sank. More came, and more. They filled the pail until it overflowed. And the water ran—south.

I opened my eyes, scarcely daring to believe what had happened. "South. He's been taken somewhere south of here. Not very far, maybe. But I'm not sure about that. Just south."

Tu's little lipless mouth hadn't smiled a lot. But now it did. "South. Let us go!"

He sounded a lot more confident than I felt. This psychic stuff was weird. Maybe my mind was just making it all up. And anyway, there's a

lot of stuff south of here. Mexico, for example.
And Argentina and places like that.

Anyway, we left the room, locking the door
behind us. Soon we were standing on the sidewalk in front of the hotel. I was surprised to
see that it was almost dark. But that shouldn't
complicate things. Roswell was laid out in a
simple grid. Main Street ran south and north.
We turned south and started walking.

I wondered if my sense of my dad would lead
me right or left when we got closer to him. Or
would I have to go through the whole garbage
pail thing. Could I even make it work again?

Main Street ahead of us was getting more
and more crowded. Suddenly, the streetlights
turned off. All of them. As far as we could see
down the length of Main Street, they were all
off. That was odd. There was still a lot of light
ahead of us, but it was bobbing and weaving
through the street.

Then I remembered. The nighttime parade. A
crowd was lining the sidewalk now. The parade
was already well underway. People wearing crazy

costumes marched down the street. They had glow sticks looped around their necks and arms. Old guys rode miniature cars lit with Christmas lights. They were driving madly around in interweaving formations. I knew we didn't have time to stop and watch. But I couldn't help looking through gaps in the crowd as we walked quickly behind them. A high school band marched by, loudly playing the *Star Wars* theme. They were draped with glow sticks and had flashlights tied to their heads.

Then came a pickup truck float. The people on the back were all dressed as *Star Wars* characters. Darth Vader and Luke Skywalker fought with glowing toy light sabers. A storm trooper fought with a hooded Obi Wan Kenobi. Princess Leia, Yoda, and Chewbacca skipped along behind the truck. They were handing out candy to kids.

It was crazy and funny. Everyone was enjoying themselves. Everyone except the two real aliens hurrying along the sidewalk.

Suddenly, I was enjoying myself even less. We were crossing a side street. Cars were stopped by barriers for the parade. One of those drivers was cursing as he abandoned his car. Then he started walking along the sidewalk toward us. Our gazes locked. It was Major Garrett.

"Run!" I whispered, grabbing Tu's hand.

There was nowhere to run but into the crowd and the advancing parade. People dressed as storm troopers and Jawas were marching raggedly along after the *Star Wars* float. Behind them came another float. A flatbed truck all lit up with blinking white and green Christmas lights. All the riders were dressed like various, wild sorts of aliens. I recognized a few from the costume contest.

We screeched to a halt while that float rolled past. An idea hit me like a laser. With Tu in tow, I ran around behind that float and up along the far side. Grabbing the edge of the flatbed, I pulled Tu and myself up onto it. Tu's hat tumbled off as we wedged ourselves in between the spangly four-armed woman and a large, winged lizard man. The woman looked down at Tu and grinned.

"Our real contest winner! Welcome aboard, kid. I bet you weren't supposed to ride in the parade either."

I grinned back at her. "Right. But we just couldn't miss it."

The marching band coming along behind us was blaring *Star Trek* music. It clashed wildly with the *Star Wars* music in front. Nobody minded. Tu and I scrunched ourselves way down. We hoped the spangly woman's extra arms and the lizard guy's wings would help hide us.

Now came motorcycle riders in black leather jackets decorated with green aliens. They zoomed up and down along the sides of several floats. Hopefully, Garrett hadn't seen us jump onto this float. But if he had, the motorcycles were an added defense.

Most of the cycles were brightly painted and shiny with chrome. The one riding along beside us now was the exception. It was old and rusty. The short guy riding it had a bristly gray beard sticking from under the face guard of his battered helmet.

With a growl of gears, the rider inched his cycle closer. He reached out one black-gloved hand toward us.

"Tu!" he cried. "Jump on. Your friend too."

Tu started to move, but I held him back. Who was this guy?

"Jump on!" the man repeated. "Tu, I am your father!"

CHAPTER SIX

It was like some acrobatic circus act. Tu leaped from the moving float onto the back of the moving motorcycle. I had no choice but to follow. Good thing there was a lot of space on that back seat. Even so, we were all three scrunched up. I was gripping Tu's waist. He was gripping his dad's. Tu's father! We'd found him. Or rather, he'd found us. That psychic connection thing must really work!

The driver gunned the cycle. Expertly we dodged in and out of parade marchers and floats. We'd nearly reached the beginning of the parade when we abruptly turned left and jutted off onto a side street. Then came a maze of streets and alleys that I only half saw in the dark. Away from Main Street and the parade, widely spaced streetlights were still on.

We bumped over a weedy lawn and abruptly dropped into the concrete bed of a canal. Water filled only the trough down its center. A path ran alongside. Rolling along that path, we were well below ground level. We'd be out of sight of any pursuers, if we hadn't already lost them.

For a moment, I glimpsed a full moon rising in the east. Then it was blotted out by the approaching dark span of a railroad bridge. The cycle slowed as we moved under the slanting beams and uprights of the bridge. The motor coughed into silence.

"Off," the driver ordered. Immediately he rolled the cycle into concealing shadows. Then he turned and reached out both hands for Tu's. They simply held on, staring silently into each other's eyes. Psychic talking, I guessed.

An intruder at a long overdue reunion, I moved away. Climbing a few steps up the steep slanting wall of the canal, I sat down. Then I leaned against a beam that smelled of the oily stuff that summer heat bakes out of old railroad lumber.

Frogs and crickets filled the night with rhythmic chirping. The sounds of the town and the parade were a distant jangle. A pigeon, disturbed by our arrival, cooed its complaint from a nest in the beams overhead. But the lulling sounds did nothing to ease my tension and fear. I thought about my own father.

At last the two Nythians stirred. The elder stepped toward me. "Thank you for helping my son," he said. "I am Iv. I sensed Tu was suddenly near, here on Earth. It has been hard to find him in these crowds. Come, let us sit down and talk briefly. I know you must be anxious about your own father. But there is much that each of us needs to know."

We settled onto the cold, litter-strewn concrete beside the shallow canal. Light from a distant streetlight reached us from the west. The newly risen moon shone from the east. By that mixed light, Iv looked like a short bearded human. He was taller than Tu but not taller than me. Then he reached up and gingerly tugged on his beard. Slowly it peeled off.

"Sheep wool," he laughed. "This wool, a few good human friends, and some tanning cream. They all helped me pass as a grizzled, old ranch hand over the years."

I was overwhelmed. Here was the answer to what all those UFO fans had been asking for so long. I wanted to know everything. But there was only time for a few questions. "So you survived the crash and got taken to the military base. But how did you get away?"

"I was not badly hurt," Iv said, "unlike my fellows. But I pretended to be so that maybe my captors would not be as watchful. Still, it would have been nearly impossible to escape except for one kind human nurse. She felt sorry for me, a captive in a very strange land. She did not want to see me probed and caged like some laboratory animal. She helped me get out of that building and off the base. I never saw her again. I later learned that she had been sent away. Then a few months later, she was mysteriously killed. I will always feel sorry if I brought that upon her."

For a while we were silent. Then Iv continued. "I hid out for a while in the scrublands, in ditches, under bushes, in abandoned ranch buildings. It was in one of those that I met my other good human friend, Joe Rainmaker. He was just a boy then. His father worked on one of the ranches. Joe did not want soldiers or police to find me any more than I did. He helped disguise and hide me. He taught me enough language and local ways to pass as an old drifter, doing odd jobs. He grew up and has died now. Sadly, humans have such short life spans. But he left me his old motorcycle and good memories."

"And you stayed around Roswell all this time?" I asked.

"Oh yes. I knew that eventually someone would come for me. I hoped it would be Tu."

He smiled at his son. "And I found it amusing to see how the story of our crash grew into a legend. And now it is cause for great local celebration. I always come to these festivals. Humans are so curious, serious, and fun-loving all at the same time. And they can be very persistent too. Like your Major Garrett."

I tensed. "You know that guy? Do you know what he's done with my dad?"

"Garrett's father was one of those army officers first involved in covering up the Roswell crash. He knew that one of us had survived and escaped. He passed that information on to his son. That son also went into the army. Now the father is dead. And though the son is retired, he has made it his life's work to keep the truth of the crash from the public. He also wants to prove it to the government. That is why he seeks me."

"So why kidnap my dad?"

"From what Tu tells me, Garrett must think your father is protecting me. When he saw Tu with you, he must have thought that he had found the missing alien. But do I understand that your father knows nothing of all this?"

I moaned. "He doesn't know why we're really here or what I really am. And he's in deep trouble, just the same! I've got to help him! Do you know where he can be?"

Iv nodded his head. Like his son's, it looked too large to be supported by his spindly neck. "I can guess. After retiring, Garrett came back to Roswell and bought a home. He wanted to keep looking for evidence of me. Once, for fun, I stopped by and offered to do some odd jobs around his place. He did not recognize me, but his guard dog did. I get along with most Earth animals just fine. But not dogs. They do not seem to like the smell of Nythians. I did not accept that handyman job. I am guessing that Garrett took your father there and locked him up. Then he went out looking for you and your alien companion."

I jumped up. "Can you tell me where it is?"

"It would be easier to show you. Besides, Tu and I can not fly off home and leave you and

your father in this mess. After all, you managed to keep Tu safe until we could finally find
each other."

I felt a wave of gratitude. It seemed that
Nythians, humans, and my species all shared
some of the same values.

Mounting the motorcycle again, we retraced
our route until the canal met a street. Then
we headed south. It was harder to focus my
feelings now. I did have a vague sense that
we were getting closer to my dad. We avoided
the main streets. Iv had lived in this area
longer than most of its human residents. He
knew every back road and overgrown trail.
Soon, we were way south of town, near the
airport. The houses were mostly small and a
little rundown. A big tangle of willow trees
hung over the gravel road, where Iv finally
stopped the cycle.

"This is Garrett's place," he said, pointing to
a fenced yard. Through the screen of bushes,
moonlight showed a low, building. Lights
glowed in several of the windows.

"My dad's there?"

"It is the only building on the property where he could lock somebody up. Do you feel your dad is there?"

I closed my eyes. I felt too tense to do the emptying mind trick. But I did sort of catch a mental whiff of something Dad-like. I also sensed something else. Dog.

"Yes, I *think* he's there. But I also think there's a dog about."

Iv shook his head. "Then Tu and I had better not go in. How do you get along with dogs?"

I thought a moment. The translator stuck in my ear allowed me to understand other species. It had been intended for communicating with aliens. But on my last assignment, I'd found it worked for other Earth species as well. It had worked on horses and a vulture. Later, around our home neighborhood, I'd tried it on a few dogs and cats. With animals I didn't actually have to talk "horse" or "dog" or whatever. It kind of worked on a mental level.

"I guess I'm okay with them," I answered. "Just so they don't bite first and ask questions later."

"Good. Climb over the fence and get near the house. If your dad is alone, maybe you can talk with him. Maybe even break him out. If Garrett or others are there too, maybe you can listen in and figure out what their plans are. We will be here waiting."

"How can I . . . "

Tu was already digging in one of the little packets on his belt. "I have got some items you might need. Here is a tool that cuts and does other useful things."

He handed me a small, silvery tool that looked like a nail clipper. I slipped it into a pocket.

"And here is a communicator. Just stick it on your cheek between your mouth and your ear. I will wear one too. Talk or whisper. We will be able to hear each other."

Cautiously I pressed a smooth bluish disk against my cheek. It stuck as if glued.

As Iv rolled the motorcycle further into the shadow of the willow, I eyed the fence. Chain link, maybe eight-feet high. This guy sure didn't look like a friendly neighbor. Fortunately, I'd learned that climbing was one of my alien skills. That had surprised and even scared me at first. Now it came almost naturally. Almost.

Taking a deep breath, I wedged the toe of my shoe into one of the diamond-shaped gaps. Trying not to think, I scrambled up, over, and down the far side. Smiling more confidently than I felt at Tu and Iv, I slipped off through the brush-choked yard.

The only sounds around me were night chirpings and a few twigs crackling under my feet. Then came a growl like from a saber-toothed tiger. The black shape in front of me looked as big as a compact car. Teeth and eyes glinted in the moonlight. Words buzzed in my translator. Mostly they had to do with anger and tearing things apart.

CHAPTER SEVEN

"Nice doggie," was my first quavering thought. But I had to do better than that. Fast.

"Oh good, you're free," I said in my mind. "I was afraid that mean human of yours was keeping you chained."

The thought that came back felt confused but still basically vicious. "Free? Free to tear you apart."

"No! Free to come over and have your tummy rubbed. You're such a fine dog. You deserve better than the treatment you're given. I bet that mean Major Garrett never rubs your tummy."

"No. Doesn't."

"Come here. I love rubbing tummies of hand-some, strong dogs." Slowly the dark shape slunk nearer. The tail began to wag. With a grunt, the huge dog dropped to the ground and rolled on his back.

I spent the next five minutes rubbing dog tummy, ears, and chest. This big guy smelled strongly of dog. Dog that hadn't had a doggie bath in months. Finally I stood up. "Now I want to see where you live. For a grand dog like you, it must be a grand place."

"Isn't." But the dog heaved himself to his feet. He padded off toward the building that squatted in the center of the weedy lot. I could see now that it was a grounded mobile home.

"Hold it," I thought at the dog. "We'd better be kind of sneaky, so your human doesn't think I'm here to offer you a better home. Of course I could, but I wouldn't want to tempt you to be disloyal. A noble dog like you wouldn't desert his human. Even a mean human."

The dog just grunted in reply. But he switched to a route that avoided the windows. "Here," he thought at me when he reached a rundown dog house. A ratty rug spilled out of it.

"Oh, he should do better by you than that." I tried to put a lot of sadness into my thoughts. It wasn't all an act. Garrett didn't seem like your best dog owner. Looking around, I pointed to where the mobile home was raised up on squat cinderblocks. "I bet it's a lot cozier under there."

"Is. Want to see?"

"Yes, please!"

Eagerly now, the dog led me to the back end of the trailer. He dropped to the dusty ground and began crawling under. I followed, awkwardly shuffling through dust, filth, and the thick odor of dog and mold. The floor of the trailer, only three feet off the ground, trailed sticky spider webs. That didn't matter. The important thing was that I could hear voices through it. When I got right underneath them, I stopped. The dog cuddled in beside me, rolled over, and presented his tummy for rubbing. I rubbed and listened.

"Admit it," a harsh voice said. Major Garrett's, I thought. "No point denying anything now, Mister. I've seen how your coconspirator whisked your son and the alien away on a motorcycle. I'll get them eventually. But it would save a lot of time and trouble if you confess your part in this plot."

I recognized my dad's voice next. My heart hurt for him.

"I can't confess, because I'm not part of any plot! I've told you that again and again. Wave that gun at me all you want, but this is all some ridiculous mistake. My son doesn't know about any aliens either. Not real ones. He's just enjoying this crazy festival."

Garrett laughed gruffly. "That's just what you people want us to think, isn't it? That the whole Roswell crash thing was made up as a tourist gimmick for the puny town of Roswell. Well, I know the truth, Mister, and soon I'll be able to prove it."

My dad's voice sounded tired. "Look, you've told me that whole story already. About carrying on your father's mission to find evidence of a supposed missing alien. But you're retired from the military now. You can give up this obsession. Get some professional help, why don't you? Admit that this is some paranoid delusion of yours. Or maybe that someone is playing a cruel hoax on you."

My dog-tummy rubbing had slowed to a stop, but a rumbling whine set me working again. Above me, Garrett's laugh sounded anything but good-natured. "Forget the psychoanalysis. I'm retired in name only. The military isn't all pulled out of Roswell, even if the old base is closed. And I still have plenty of contacts. They know I'm the go-to man for anything dealing with UFOs.

"Now, start talking, or I'll turn you over to the non-retired military. They won't be so gentle in their questioning. I can promise you that."

"Go ahead. Do it," my dad said. "Turn me over to the military. To the police. Anything!

It's better than being in the hands of a lunatic. Using duct tape to tie me to a chair! It's like some melodramatic spy movie!"

"Look, Mister, if you don't . . . "

A cell phone jingled a musical march in what sounded like another room. Overhead, footsteps clomped that way. This might be my chance! If I could cut a hole in the trailer's floor with Tu's gizmo, maybe I could spring my dad. But I'd have to work fast. Garrett's phone call had better be a long one.

With my non-tummy-rubbing hand, I pulled the little silver device from my pocket. I stuck it against the metal flooring above my head. Just like Tu had shown me, I pushed the side knob. A faint buzzing and light produced a deep cut in the metal. I moved my hand carefully. When I'd opened a cookie-sized hole, I whispered through it.

"Dad, it's me, Zack. Hold on. I'll get you out of there." I heard a shuffling overhead, like chair legs scraping. But then came the hurried sound of footsteps returning.

"Aha!" Garrett exclaimed. "Your game's up now, Mister! I told you I still had contacts. One just called to tell me something strictly classified. It seems they tracked a UFO several days ago. It appeared to come down just east of here. And now they think they've located the ship itself. My contact suggested I come out to the site now. This could crack everything open!

"You're coming too, of course, Mister. Can't risk you escaping now. I'll cut you loose. But don't try any funny business. This gun is loaded, and I know how to use it."

There was thumping and scraping. My dad used some language he didn't usually use around me. Then over it, I heard a tinny voice coming from the communicator stuck to my cheek. I'd forgotten about that.

"Zack," Tu's voice whispered, "we heard most of what you heard. Do not try to rescue your father now. You could both end up shot. Rejoin us, and we will all follow them."

I heard a door slamming overhead. The major was taking my dad away! I crawled as fast as I could toward the end of the trailer. But Tu was right. I'd be too late and wouldn't be able to stop this anyway.

Finally, I crawled out and stood up, festooned with cobwebs and dirt. The dog stood wagging its tail beside me. On the other side of the mobile home, I heard an engine start up. Running around the trailer, I saw the red taillights of a white van. It bounced down a gravel drive toward a gate. The gate slid open, and the van, with my dad captive inside, disappeared.

Tu's tinny voice fluttered around me again. "Quick, we will meet you at the gate. They will be heading where I hid, or thought I hid, my ship. Oh, and please try tell your dog friend not to come along."

The dog was looking up at me, its great pink tongue flopping between inch-long fangs. I tried to push aside rising panic to think dog-directed thoughts. "Just like that mean guy to go off on an adventure without you. Well, it's up to you to guard the place. You're a noble dog. You'll be loyal whether he deserves it or not. Maybe when he sees that, he'll scratch your tummy more."

I was already running down the drive. The dog loped behind me a little. Then with a grumpy thought of "Right, loyal," he turned back.

The motorcycle, engine grumbling, was waiting for me. I climbed on behind Tu. With a jerk that nearly kicked me off, we sped into the night.

Agent Sorn's words from just a few days ago bounced through my mind like a jeering chant. "Easy and fun, easy and fun!" Yes, indeed. Sure sums up this assignment. Easy and fun.

CHAPTER EIGHT

We took a tangled series of rough back roads. They eventually led to a nearly deserted highway heading east. The moon was now high overhead. Its silver glow lit the landscape around us in a weird, unreal way. The daytime colors were erased. It looked as though we were driving through an old black-and-white movie.

Far ahead on the road, I could see a pair of red taillights like angry red eyes. That must be Garrett's van. And in it, my dad. My insides twisted with guilt. Talk about innocent bystanders! He was mixed up in this extreme weirdness with a madman now threatening his life. All because of me!

The flat, boring landscape that surrounded Roswell was beginning to change. Ahead of us rose a rim of hills. Beyond them, along the horizon, the starry sky was blotted out by a wall of clouds. Moonlight outlined their billowy tops. Thunderheads, it looked like. But they were still far away. A little rain would be welcome, I thought. Even at night, the air around here was hot and heavy. At the moment, though, the speed of the motorcycle cooled things a bit.

Now the road dipped down and slid across a bridge. I caught sight of a sign as we whipped past. The Pecos River. A name out of those Old West cowboy songs. I'd never expected to see it this way. Instead of an old cowboy movie, this was a science-fiction film. And, like it or not, I was one of the actors.

The road climbed into the hills. The tail-lights in front of us disappeared. Then they reappeared again and again as the road passed over ridges and into narrow gullies. But those red eyes kept looking farther and farther away. Garrett's van was obviously faster than Iv's old motorcycle. I itched with impatience. But there was nothing I could do.

I got the feeling that the two sitting in front of me were talking. It wasn't out loud. My translator seemed to work with thoughts only for creatures that couldn't speak. Creatures like dogs and horses. But for species that did speak, it seemed to only translate spoken words, not thoughts. That was probably good. I didn't like the idea of being able to burst into people's private thoughts. That might be useful, but a little creepy and rude too.

Still, I wondered what those two were saying. Catching up after sixty-some years? How's your mom? How's your schoolwork? Weird, thinking of people with lives stretched out like that. I hoped Tu was at least able to give his dad clear directions about where to find his hidden spaceship. Though if the military had already found it, maybe it wouldn't be hard to find his hidden ship.

Ahead of us stretched a line of sharp cliffs. I thought I saw the red taillights turn off to the right along the base of the cliffs. When we reached that intersection, Iv drove straight ahead. He took a road that led to the top of the cliffs.

"The van went the other way!" I called over the rushing air.

"Right," Iv called back. "But I know this area well. We will have a better view and a better chance at surprise, working from above."

Whatever. I tried to curb my doubt by looking at the landscape. It certainly was more interesting now. The cliffs were banded with what, even in the moonlight, appeared to be layers of white and red. Once we reached the ridge top, the road ran along the rim. To the east, the land was flat. It stretched off to where thunderclouds were rolling closer. Now and again, lightning flashed through them. It lit the dark mass as if a giant was using a flash camera inside.

To the west, we could see mountains in the far distance. Between us and them, the land was mostly dark. A few clusters of light showed small towns. One was probably Roswell.

For the whole trip, Iv had been driving without his headlight on. Less visible, I guess. Maybe Nythians saw better in the dark than my species or humans did. I hoped so. In spots, it seemed like we were driving awfully close to the edge of the cliff. The moonlight helped, though. And the moon moving west was still well ahead of the thunderclouds from the east.

I could see light ahead of us, seeming to rise from below the cliff. It was strong white light, like outside an over-lit shopping center. As we got nearer, Iv steered us off the paved road. We jounced for a while over rough ground near the cliff's edge. Then he stopped the motor, and we stumbled off.

"What's going on?" I whispered. The racket rising from below the cliff made whispering hardly necessary.

"It is my fault," Tu muttered unhappily. "I should have known how to fly one of those ships better. Then I would have set the deflector controls right. The military must have tracked the ship when I entered the atmosphere. Then they traced it here. And I thought I had hidden it so well!"

Iv put an arm around his son's shoulder. "I told you not to blame yourself. You are just a youngster with hardly any flight training. It is amazing that you were able to make off with a ship and fly it here at all. And those ships are made for larger crews. You could hardly hope to get all the controls right."

Tu gazed up at his dad in a way that made me hurt inside. I felt the same way about my own dad. I had to get him out of the danger I'd put him in.

Tu led us over the rough ground toward the edge of the cliff. It wasn't easy going. Low scrubby brush and spiky cactuses clutched at our legs. The ground itself was rocky and uneven. My sneakers crunched over sharp spurs of rock. Some crumbled under my feet.

"What is this stuff?" I muttered, looking down. The moonlight glinted off flecks and sheets of crystal in the rock.

"Sandstone, shot through with gypsum," Iv said. "Gypsum is something humans sometimes mine for. But this is a park. No mining allowed. Here, it just makes the rock interesting, sharp, and crumbly."

And it was good too for tearing up hands. I realized that as we reached the cliff edge and crouched down to peer over.

Below, the area was lit up like a movie set. Military trucks and jeeps were parked all over. Directly below us was a small lake. Lights on tall poles were set up around the lake. A squat generator growled away to power them. By their bright white light, the water of the lake looked a deep emerald green.

Crouched beside me, Tu said, "I hid my ship at the bottom of that lake. It is so deep you could not even see it from above. Not until the people with their detectors and lights came, anyway."

From behind a prickly bush, I peered into the water far below. There did seem to be a darker green shape down in the depths of the lake. A big crane was squatting on the lake's rim. It looked like the military was getting ready to pull the ship out. Really bad news.

But I had more worries besides having the government find an alien ship. I looked around at all the military vehicles. No white van. I strained to see beyond the glare of lights. More cars were parked farther away. One looked like it could be Garrett's van.

"It seems we have two missions here," Iv said. "Zack, your priority must to be freeing your father. Since most attention seems to be on the lake, that should be possible. Meanwhile, Tu and I will have to slip down there and get to the ship before they retrieve it. The lights will be a problem. But hopefully we can scale the cliff and slip into the water without anyone noticing. Then we can swim down to it."

Tu didn't voice any objection. I guess climbing steep cliffs and swimming way underwater were things Nythians could do. I wasn't so sure about my own task though. The climbing part wouldn't be so bad for me. But this cliff wasn't like the ones I had climbed before. The rock was sharp and really crumbly. And even if I got my dad out of that van, how could I get him back up here? He was human and couldn't do my alien climbing thing.

Tu seemed to share my doubts. "Zack, you should take my antigrav pack with you. It might help. My father and I are light enough. We will not need it for this."

He reached into one of his belt pouches and pulled out a little square object. "Pull the cord here when you need it. It expands."

Iv put a hand on my shoulder. "I want to thank you for everything, Zack. Keep up your good work here. If Tu and I do not manage this, do not distress yourself. We will not let ourselves or our ship be captured. We will blow it up and us with it, if we have to."

"No, you shouldn't . . . "

Iv interrupted. "Zack, I have been on this planet observing humans a great deal longer than you have. They are a good-hearted species but easily misled. And military people tend to look for enemies everywhere. It is their job. The people coming each year to that silly Roswell festival at least have a good attitude toward aliens. But if the military gets hold of us or that ship, they will start worrying about invasions and weapons. The general public may be way ahead of their governments in being ready to accept the existence of aliens. But government fears could poison that. Earth's readiness to join the Galactic Union could be badly harmed. We do not want to be responsible for that."

"But . . . "

"No. Go down there and get your father out of trouble. Use the motorcycle to get away if you need to. One way or another, I will not need it anymore. Go."

Without another word, he scurried north along the edge of the rim. Before Tu followed, the young Nythian turned to me. "Thank you,

Zack. You have been a great friend. I wish you well with your father. But it will all work out. Do not worry." Then he hurried after Iv.

Don't worry. Right.

A little further along the cliff, I saw them slip over the edge. They had both shed all of their human disguises. Now they were little gray people in tight gray suits. Immediately they blended into the rocky ridges and shadows and disappeared. At least I needn't worry about them being seen, not right away anyhow.

What Iv had said was right, I knew. But that didn't make me feel happier about any of this. Still, I had to free my dad. I had to do it now. Crouching low, I hurried along the edge of the cliff away from most of the white glare. Getting flat on my stomach, I peered again over the edge. The white van was Garrett's van. It was right below me, parked by itself near a twisted tree. Almost certainly Garrett had left my dad tied up inside.

I was about to lower myself over the cliff edge when an explosive boom nearly made me topple off. I rolled over, looking behind me. Thunder. The storm clouds had rolled much closer. Now instead of soft flashes, lightning showed up as quick, jagged forks. It was grand and dramatic looking, like a spectacular movie or stage set.

Great. That's just what I needed. More drama.

CHAPTER NINE

This cliff was horrible. Even for a guy like me who came from some planet where people probably climb cliffs all the time. The rock was sharp, gouging my hands and tearing through my jeans. And chunks of it kept breaking off. When I wasn't worried about falling to my death, I worried that the noise of falling rock would alert someone. But the military's generator, crane, and people shouting orders filled the night with enough noise to mask any I made.

Finally, knees shaking, I stood at the bottom, on solid ground. The moon was hidden now behind the advancing storm clouds. But frequent flashes of lightning lit up the area. Crouching behind a spindly bush, I looked around. Nobody was near. The thought of seeing a flying saucer pulled out of a lake had drawn everybody toward the lights. Still, I crouched low. Creeping from shadow to shadow, I reached the van.

A quick glance. Nobody was in the cab. My dad must be in the back. Surely Major Garrett wouldn't drag him out of the van. That would risk my dad escaping with all that UFO information he supposedly had.

I moved to the back of the van and tried the handle. Locked. I rapped on the door. Nothing. I rapped again. Something shuffled inside. I heard a muffled voice.

"It's me, Dad. I'll get you out," I called softly, pulling the silver cutting tool from my pocket. More mumbling from inside.

Thumbing the dial on the cutter, I sliced a neat circle through the metal near the door handle. Clumsily I caught the chunk of metal as it fell away. Reaching inside, I opened the latch. The door swung open, revealing darkness inside. Darkness and an even darker shape inching forward like a giant caterpillar.

"Dad!" I scrambled inside and pulled him closer to the door. His arms and legs were bound with duct tape. He had another strip across his mouth. That's what I pulled off first.

"Ouch!" he gasped but instantly was grinning. "Zack. Am I ever glad to see you! What . . . "

"I know you've got questions, Dad," I said hurriedly. "But let's get you out of here first."

Using the cutting tool, I carefully sliced through the tape on his ankles and wrists. Then I helped him out of the van. He wobbled at first. His feet were half asleep.

"We've got to get away from here and up the cliff. Then we can talk."

Still alone in this darkened area, we quickly hobbled over to the base of the cliff. My dad looked curiously to where the harsh lights lit up the rock towering over the deep lake. "What's going on there? Is that where they found this supposed spaceship?"

"Yeah, but it's a real spaceship. More later."
I pulled from my pocket the little square packet
that Tu had given me. "This cliff is nasty to
climb. Let's see if we can get this antigravity
thing to work."

I pulled the cord. With a hiss, the little
square expanded and bulged out in places.
When it stopped changing, I saw there were
two straps hanging from a black metallic oval.
It looked like a flabby football. Ignoring my
dad's questions, I helped him slip his arms
into the straps. Just putting it onto someone
seemed to trigger a mechanism. A dial glowed.
With a yelp, my dad was lifted slightly off
the ground.

"Whoa! Incredible. I feel almost weightless."

"Good. That should help. Now hold tight to
my belt. I'll do the climbing."

I began to climb. The climb up was worse
than the one down. Every time a bit of cliff
broke away, my dad gasped. He clutched my
belt and shoulders, throwing me off balance
even more. Halfway up, a ledge we were

crouching on suddenly crumbled and slid down the cliff in a shower of rock and pebbles. My dad flailed in panic.

Digging my fingers into tiny crevasses in the rock, I hissed, "Hold still!"

He did. For moments, we hung motionless, plastered to the cliff face. Nobody over at the noisy lighted area acted as if they had heard. The almost constant rumbling of thunder over-head helped as well. My fingers ached from holding my own weight and the little that my dad still had. No light was shone our way. Taking a deep breath, I fumbled for new foot-holds. Again I began scrambling up.

I noticed something wet running down my face. I figured it was blood from some rock cut on my forehead. Then I felt wet on my hands and the top of my head. It was starting to rain. Great.

Finally, gasping and wheezing, I hauled us over the cliff top. Dad let go of my belt. Quickly he grabbed it again as he started drifting upward. I yanked him down. Then I rolled over and struggled to get him out of the antigrav pack. I didn't know how to shrink it again. But pulling the same cord sent it shriveling back into a little square packet.

"Cool," I whispered, then stuffed the thing back into my pocket. I looked at my dad. He had crawled away from the cliff edge but was now sitting staring at me.

"Explanation time?" he said quietly.

This was it. The moment I'd been dreading for months. Lies weren't an option now. After all, I'd just scrambled up a cliff in a very non-human way. It was truth time. And suddenly I was glad.

"Right..." I paused a long time then jumped into it. "I know I was adopted."

"You know..."

"Yes, but that's not the big secret. I've no problem with the adoption thing. I'm okay with that, really. But last year, I learned that though you and Mom thought you'd adopted a human baby, you hadn't. I'm actually an alien. You know, like from another planet. I was put here by folks in the Galactic Union, a big space organization. They wanted me to grow up in a regular human family, so I could do some work for them later."

Dad almost choked for a moment then managed to whisper, "My son? An alien?" Then taking a deep breath, he looked at me. "So all that UFO stuff Major Garrett was babbling on about was... true?"

"Some of it was. Yes, there was a Roswell UFO crash and a survivor. Though as it turns out, the Galactic Union didn't know that last part. The real reason I was sent to New Mexico was to try to find this guy's son. He had stolen a spaceship and flew here to try to locate his dad."

My dad groaned. "You know, if I wasn't sitting in the rain on top of a cliff in New Mexico, having just been hauled up by someone who climbs like a lizard, I'd laugh. Laugh hysterically, probably. You're my son, for crying out loud!"

Desperately I hugged him. "Yes, I am your son! I love you. You raised me." Laughter seemed to threaten me too. "I just came from a different kind of adoption agency."

It was beginning to rain more seriously now, washing away the fresh smell of rain on warm rock. My dad shook the dripping hair out of his eyes. "Shouldn't we find someplace a little more sheltered to talk?"

"We can't yet. Tu and Iv, the two aliens I told you about, have sneaked down there. They're trying to get their spaceship out of the lake before the military claims it. I need to stick around. Maybe I can help or at least report what happened."

Crouching beside me in the rain, I could feel my dad shrug. "Whatever you say. I couldn't get much wetter anyway."

We inched closer to the cliff edge and looked down on the activity around the little lake. Some of the figures below seemed to be trying to get out of the rain. Most were ignoring it, concentrating on the winch cable that was being lowered into the water. Three people in black diving suits walked toward the lake. One by one, they tested the water then slipped in.

Where were Tu and Iv? Had they managed to climb down the cliff all right? Had they been able to swim unnoticed to the ship? And what would happen if the divers got there too? What if they managed to hook all their cables around the Nythian ship?

"So . . . what exactly is supposed to happen?" my dad said. "Are your friends going to shoot all those people with ray guns or some such?"

"No, I don't think Nythians do things like that. Besides, the idea is to create as little proof as possible that there are aliens here."

Overhead, thunder and lightning exploded at once. Instantly, the air around us smelled like a bad chemistry experiment. We both threw hands over our heads and buried our faces in the now muddy ground.

When we could breathe again, my dad said shakily, "The experts say you're supposed to lie low when caught in a thunderstorm. I suppose we can't get much lower than flat on our faces."

I stared again over the edge. The divers had dropped beneath the surface. The winch cables were slowly being lowered.

Dad said what I was thinking. "If your friends are really nonviolent types, they'd better act quickly. Those people will have things hooked up soon. And notice the soldiers standing around. They're all armed. They won't take kindly to a couple of space people trying to hijack their prize. But your friends don't have much hope of secrecy with all that light focused on the lake."

The light, I'd realized. That was the problem. If I could do something about the light . . .

"Dad, do you have your cell phone on you? No, right. I saw it smashed at the hotel." Frantically I began patting at my pockets, but mine was gone as well. Probably fell out when I was doing my cliff-climbing.

I growled in frustration. "I need something with a power source. This is a crazy idea but . . . oh, wait, maybe this gizmo will work."

"What are you going to do?"

"I'm not sure," I said, pulling Tu's cutting tool out of a pocket I'd had the good sense to snap shut. "I've done something like this before, but usually by accident. And even though I've been practicing in the back yard . . . Eh, sorry about the brick wall I put holes in."

"That was you? No, never mind. Go on."

"Well, I'm still not sure exactly how I do this. But here goes."

Closing my eyes, I tried to drain my mind of all extra thoughts. I tried to feel like rain was washing down inside my head as well as outside. Holding the little tool in front of me, I focused my thoughts on its tiny power cell. I felt the tingle of its power. I let that power reach into me and touch the power that lay waiting in every cell of my body.

That's what I tried to do, anyway. It didn't seem to work at first. I felt foolish trying this freaky alien thing with my dad right there watching. But then I thought of Tu and his dad. They were two innocent people about to see their way home cut off, their ship snatched by soldiers, maybe themselves captured . . . or shot.

The power sizzled in my cells, straining to get out. I let it loose. The tool I held began to glow.

The glow spread to my hand. It ran up my arm. I thought I heard my dad gasp beside me. But all my attention was on the picture in my mind, the picture of the exact arc I wanted my throw to follow. Drawing my arm back, I threw the tool into the night.

Then it felt and looked like the world had come to an end.

CHAPTER TEN

I sagged against my dad. As usual, this sort of thing totally wiped me out. But I didn't pass out this time. Good thing, or I would have missed quite a show.

Through blurry eyes, I watched the little glowing speck sail along that perfect arc right toward the electric generator. I had hoped to maybe short it out somehow. What I got was far more.

I didn't see the little tool hit, but I did see the effect. A jagged electric net suddenly snaked over the generator. It leaped across to the light poles and shot up them. The lights flickered but didn't go out. Not until the lightning struck.

Power called to power. A sizzling spear of lightning jabbed from the clouds into the equipment below. There was a horrendous explosion. Everything went dark.

My dad and I squinted through the rain. A few flashlight beams crisscrossed the area below us, showing glimpses of people. They were running for the cars or out into the desert. Anywhere to be away from the smoldering generator and lights. I didn't see any bodies lying around, though, and breathed a sigh of relief.

Then there was something else to see. The little lake began to glow green. Something seemed to rise from the depths. Three panicky figures in wetsuits scrambled from the water and fled. The shape kept coming. It was a glowing silver spaceship. Not really saucer-shaped, it looked more like an inflated spearhead. Then it burst from the water and hovered over the surface for a moment. Water dripped off it in glittering curtains.

A few soldiers recovered themselves enough to fire their rifles at the thing. Bullets binged harmlessly off the surface. Then abruptly the ship shot straight into the air. It changed course and skimmed right over the cliff top— and our heads.

My dad had flattened himself to the ground, but I pulled him to his feet. Together we pelted through the pounding rain toward the cliff top road. Parked neatly on the pavement was the glowing silver spaceship.

A door slid open. Iv stepped into the lighted doorway. "Going my way?" he asked. Then he gave a high-pitched Nythian laugh. "I have seen a lot of movies since being here, but that was the best escape scene ever!"

I hurried up the short ramp, then turned back to look at my dad. He had the terrified, determined look of someone about to dive off a very high diving board. He shrugged, swallowed, and followed me.

Inside, the ship's walls were rounded and dotted with lights, dials, and glowing screens.

But it didn't seem as busy and cramped as an airliner cockpit. There were several small seats in front of lighted control panels and others dotted around the cabin. They all looked like under-filled water balloons. Tu offered us two along the side. We sat, although the seats were clearly meant for smaller people than my dad and me.

"We should do the formal human-introduction thing," Iv said, shaking my dad's hand. "But we had better get underway before those people try shooting missiles or something at us. I just want you to know, sir, that your son has been great. He is a fine asset to your planet. You should be proud of him."

Dad looked at me. "I am, you know. I don't really understand much of this. But pride? I've got that."

I smiled back at him.

"Come on, Tu," his dad said. "I will show you how to set the detection deflectors." For a few minutes, those two worked over one of the glowing panels, talking without words. My dad and I talked the usual way.

"Zack," he began, "can you assure me, one more time, that this is real? That this isn't some demented dream or elaborate hoax set up by the UFO festival people?"

"Yes, it is. I mean, it's real and not some dream or hoax."

He sighed. "Right. So when you get the opportunity, you'll explain everything to me? And to your mother?"

Before I could fumble out an answer that I didn't have, Iv was back with us. "Zack, if you need to follow the Galactic Union's secrecy rules you could always do that Obi Wan Kenobi thing. You know, the mental trick to make people forget what they have just seen."

I stared at him. "Hey, that was a movie. I can't do stuff like that."

"Of course it was a movie. One of my favorites. But that does not mean you cannot do it. If you are the species I think you are, you have all kinds of mental powers. But maybe you are not trained in it all as yet. Well, anyway, we have got to be going now. Where can we drop you two off? At your hotel in Roswell? Back in your hometown?"

I was still too stunned by the thought that Iv had an idea what species I really was. My dad answered. "Roswell for us, I think. Garrett and friends seem determined to catch themselves some aliens. So you two ought to head homeward as soon as you can."

Iv nodded and dropped into one of the seats in front of lit-up dials. Tu sat beside him and touched a knob. The ship vibrated slightly. The view screen at the front of the ship showed forward motion, though mostly it was through curtains of rain.

Finally we escaped the storm. Once out from the clouds, we could see the moon again. It was just about to set in the west. Fewer stars showed than before. The whole sky looked more like dark gray than black. Dawn must be near.

A landscape of grass and scrubby bushes whipped past beneath us as we skimmed low over the ground. Lights of a town drew closer. Suddenly, we stopped in midair and dropped straight down into a grove of trees.

"Roswell is just over there," Iv said, pointing to the view screen. "Can you walk from here?"

"Sure, no problem," I said. Then I frowned. The walk was no problem. But despite the thrill of riding in a real spaceship, some other problems had been nagging at me. "Do you have a phone or something I can use?"

"We can arrange something," Iv answered. "Whom do you want to call?"

I pulled a rumpled and damp card from a pocket. "Major Garrett. I don't know that I can do the Obi Wan Kenobi thing on him. But I do think we should talk."

Iv took the card, went to a console, and twiddled some dials. The sound of a phone ringing filled the cabin. I hurried over to the console and squeezed myself into a little chair. Clearing my throat nervously, I spoke at the little grid where Iv directed me.

A voice came on. A voice with familiar gravelly tones. "Hello. Major Garrett here."

I tried to make my voice sound deep and persuasive. "Major Garrett, we need to talk about tonight."

"What? Who's this?"

I looked at my dad, and suddenly knew what I was going to say to this other man. "I am one of those you've been dealing with the last few days. Major, you're a practical man. You can face reality. In a way, you won tonight. You proved that your father was right. There *was* a survivor of the Roswell crash. You also saw the UFO. No one could deny that it was alien."

He choked out a reply. "And you . . . you're one of those humans aiding the aliens!"

"What I am isn't important. You and your father both had two goals. One was to find the missing alien. You found him. The other was to make the government's cover-up work. You didn't want to upset the public with the knowledge that aliens have been here. And that's still what you want. Can you imagine what all those UFO fans in Roswell would do if they'd seen what you did just now? The secret that the government has been sitting on for years would be hopelessly out."

"But that sneaking alien . . . "

"He's no threat. He was lost here because of a freak accident. Now he's going home. Period. The only danger he poses is if people, lots of people, know he was here."

Garrett was silent a moment. "What's in this for you?"

I felt a little stupid for trying anything like the Obi Wan mind thing. But I tried to make my voice even deeper and smoother. I focused my mind on being convincing. "We share the same goals here. We want to keep all this from the public. And so do you. That was your father's job, and now it's your job. Aliens are no threat to Earth, but the public needs to be protected from a panicky fear that they might be. You can do that. It's your job. You're good at your job. Now just do it."

I didn't know how to hang up this thing. I gestured at Iv. He pressed something. The connection went dead.

I'd been concentrating so hard, I was suddenly shivering. Looking around at the others in the cabin, I saw my dad shake his head then slowly smile. "You *are* good at that."

I blushed. "Well, it's going to be hard to keep it all quiet; so many people were there. But mostly they were military people. And if Garrett and other military types decide it needs to be kept secret, maybe it will be. For a while at least."

As I stood up, Tu walked over to me. "When I get home, some Galactic Union people will probably come to Nythia. They'll yell at me for stealing a ship and coming here. But I will tell them there is nothing to worry about. They have got an excellent agent on this planet." Solemnly he shook my hand. "Thank you for being my friend."

There were more words of farewell. But we all knew that the Nythians had better get away before the military tracked them down. No matter what I'd said, I was sure Garrett's dream would still be to actually catch them.

In minutes, my father and I were standing on the scrubby outskirts of a small New Mexican town, looking into the sky. The remnants of storm clouds were turning pink with dawn. Rising into them, a silvery spaceship hovered a moment, bobbed once, and then shot off at an incredible speed. In moments, it was gone.

CHAPTER ELEVEN

Dad and I turned and headed back into Roswell. "So what now?" he said as we reached the first gravel road. It felt strange to have him, the adult, asking me for direction.

"Go to the hotel, collect our things, and get out on the first flight home? But if you still want to go off camping together, we can do that too."

Smiling wanly, he shook his head. "Thanks, but I believe I've had all the thrilling adventure I need for the moment."

I nodded. That was an understatement for both of us. "Garrett may try to track us down sometime but probably not for a while. So yes, I think it's time to go. My work here looks like it's done."

"And maybe on the flight back you'll tell me a little about that work?"

I felt incredibly guilty. "Dad, I am so sorry about all the lies. I learned about this whole thing, who I am and all, just a year ago. The Galactic Union swore me to total secrecy. That made sense, I guess. But I hated not talking to you and Mom about it." I glanced at him a moment, then looked away. "Besides, I really wasn't sure how you'd take it. I was afraid . . . well, that you might . . . "

"Might get freaked out at having a space alien for a son and send you back?" He grabbed my shoulders and looked me in the eye. "Not remotely possible, Zack. Your mom and I always knew you were special. We just thought you were special in a human kind of way. You're still our kid."

Flooded with relief, I grinned back at him. "So how are we going to break this to Mom?"

We started walking again. "Well, she won't have the easy introduction that I had. Getting kidnapped, tied up with duct tape, and fed wild stories about aliens. Then being rescued by a son who hauls people up cliffs like a lizard and fights off the military with lightning. To say nothing of a little ride in a spaceship. But somehow, we'll manage to convince her."

Then he stopped and looked at me again. "That is, unless you plan to try your mind thing on me."

I shook my head. "No. Even if I knew for sure *how* to do that, I wouldn't try it on you. Whatever the Galactic Union people say, I'm through lying to you. You're my family . . . if you'll still have me."

His hug was all the answer I needed.

When we reached Main Street, the sun hadn't risen yet, but there were already a few people about. One young man in a running suit jogged by. When he saw us, he stopped and said excitedly, "You just walked in from the east? Did you see it? I swear I saw a flying saucer!

It just took off from outside town and then zapped off through the clouds! Did you see it?"

My dad and I both looked at each other and shook our heads. "No," we said together.

"Too bad! Well, I'm sure some others must have. Wow, this is so incredible!"

After the guy jogged on, my dad said. "Does this risk your secrecy thing?"

I thought a minute. I should be worried about that, but I wasn't. I remembered what Iv had said, and a bunch of things suddenly fell into place. "I don't think so. People come here because they believe in UFOs. Because they *want* to believe in UFOs. Nobody outside will believe them if they say they actually saw one."

As we walked along Main Street, I felt tired but happy. "You know, I've just realized how great this is. That guy saw a UFO and was excited. He was happy, not afraid. All of these people at this festival have been like that. They want to believe in UFOs, in aliens who are curious about Earth maybe but don't want to invade it. And I bet that a lot of other people feel the same.

"That's where the military folks have it all wrong," I continued. "Unless something really bad happens—like some of the problems the Galactic Union assigned me to fix—the public won't panic when they learn the truth about UFOs and aliens from other planets. Most may even welcome it or at least may not be very surprised."

"But you still want Garrett and his gang to continue the cover-up?" Dad asked.

"For now, yes. The Galactic Union thinks Earth isn't quite ready to join. But I think it's probably Earth's governments, not the general public, that are the big problem. I mean, if they react to aliens like they often react to other countries, we could have real trouble. Governments are probably the ones who are most afraid. They need to cover up the truth from themselves more than from their citizens."

There were more people on the streets now. Just ahead of us, the jogger had stopped and was talking excitedly to a group of early-rising festivalgoers.

One cute teenage girl was almost bouncing up and down. "Oh, you are *so* lucky! I'd give *anything* to see a real UFO. I'd *so* love to meet an alien!"

She spun around as we approached and threw me a dazzling smile. "Wouldn't you?"

"Mm. . . me?" I stammered. "Why, yeah, that would be cool. *So* cool."

My dad chuckled as we walked on, but my mind was still on the girl behind us. A really cute girl. Sure this job of mine had its bad points. There was scary, dangerous stuff and lots of chances to get killed. But it could have its good side too.

No, this had hardly been my career choice. But all things considered, being an alien agent promised a very interesting future.

alien contact

BOOK #5 OF THE
[alien agent]
series

pamela F. service

illustrated by mike gorman

TOP SECRET from *Alien Contact*

The alarm shrilled through the little spaceship. Agent Sorn spun around and stared at the screen. A ship was pursuing hers and closing in fast. Frowning, she studied the image. A Syndicate ship. Can't be good, she thought, and accelerated full out.

Her pursuer was still closing the gap. Sorn fumed with frustration.

Here she was on a routine mission to planet Earth. The job was so routine, in fact, that she had decided to handle it herself rather than bother their planted alien agent with it. She still felt guilty about how Agent Zack had been forced to learn about his real nature and take on dangerous missions before he'd had a chance to grow up, before he'd even been fully trained. Sorn decided she'd handle this simple job herself and let Zack enjoy a little more time as an almost normal, human-looking kid.

But suddenly things did not look routine. Her little ship was now going as fast as it could, but the Syndicate ship was still gaining. Grumbling, Sorn turned to her communicator. Quickly, she wrote a message to Galactic Union Headquarters—a distress call—typing in her coordinates, her mission, and (although she hated to do it) a call for help.

She jabbed the Send button just as a golden energy glow enveloped her ship. The enemy ship was grappling hers, pulling it in. Did her distress call get off in time?

about the author

Pamela F. Service has authored more than twenty books in the science-fiction, fantasy, and nonfiction genres. After working as a history museum curator for many years in Indiana, she became the director of a museum in Eureka, California, where she lives with her husband and cats. She is also active in community theater, politics, and beachcombing.